Jalk ☆ MAGIC LEMONADE

Written by
Joyce Dunbar

Illustrated by
Jan McCafferty

BLue Bananas

For Madeline,
Edward and Grace
J.D.

For Andy
love J.M.

Zoe tottered into the yard. She was wearing high heels.

'Today I am a queen,' she announced.

'How can you be a queen? You are not dressed like a queen,' said Sam.

Zoe took a tablecloth from the washing-line. She took some clothes-pegs as well.

She wrapped the tablecloth around herself and pinned it with the pegs.

'There! Now I am dressed like a queen,'
said Zoe.

'How can you be a queen? You do not
have a crown like a queen,' said Joe.

7

'I do have a crown,' said Zoe. 'I forgot to put it on. Dee! Will you pass me the peg bag!'

Dee passed the peg bag to Zoe.

'You make a silly queen,' laughed Sam.

Zoe took some pegs out of the peg bag.

She took two white pegs, three blue

pegs and five pink pegs.

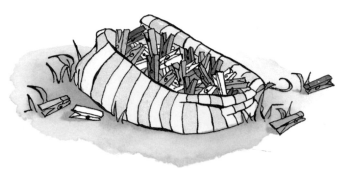

She pegged them on to her hairband.

'There! Now I have a crown!' said Zoe.

Perfect!

'And I am not a silly queen. I am a splendid queen.'

'You are not a queen, you do not have a throne to sit on,' said Joe.

'I do have a throne,' said Zoe. 'But it is not a throne to sit on. It is a throne to stand on.'

13

She climbed on to the wooden steps.
Her tablecloth gown hung down to the
ground. Her crown of pegs reached high.

'There!' said Zoe. 'I am a tall and stately queen on my throne! You must all do as I say!'

'We don't want to play queens,' said Joe.

'We are going on a snail hunt with Todd.'

'Good,' said Zoe. 'I order you to go on a snail hunt!'

Off you go!

'Then we won't go on a snail hunt,' said Sam. 'We will play conga-bonga instead.'

'Good!' said Zoe. 'I order you to play
conga-bonga instead. The Queen will
come to visit.'

'Then we won't play conga-bonga,' said Joe.

Joe and Sam and Dee started to walk away.

'I banish you from my kingdom,' said Zoe.

'We were going anyway!' said Joe.

Zoe climbed down from the wooden steps and tottered over to the old water pump. She worked the handle up and down.

'Roll up! Roll up!' shouted Zoe. 'Roll up for magic lemonade!'

Joe and Sam and Dee came back.

'What magic lemonade?' asked Sam.

'Magic lemonade from the magic
lemonade pump,' said Zoe.

'That isn't a magic lemonade pump,' said Dee. 'That's an old water pump and it doesn't even have any water.'

'Maybe not,' said Zoe. 'But when a queen works the handle, magic lemonade comes out.'

24

'Where?' said Sam.

Zoe worked the handle again.

25

'There!' said Zoe. 'Magic lemonade!'

She cupped her hands under the pump
and tasted some.

'Mmmm! Delicious!'

'There is no lemonade! There isn't
anything at all,' said Sam.

'Can't you see the magic lemonade?' said Zoe. 'Can't you hear the lemonade splashing? Can't you taste the magic lemonade?'

'There is no lemonade,' said Sam.

It fizzes!

'That's because you don't believe I'm a queen,' said Zoe. 'If you believed that I really was a queen, you would hear the magic lemonade . . .

. . . you would see the magic lemonade.

You would taste the magic lemonade.

You could all have a drink of the magic

lemonade.'

Joe and Sam and Dee licked their lips.

Zoe was making them thirsty.

'But first, you've got to believe I'm a
queen,' said Zoe.

Every inch
a queen.

'All right then, we believe you,' said Dee.

'Really, really?' said Zoe.

'Really, really,' said Dee.

'Say Your Majesty,' said Zoe.

'Your Majesty,' said Dee and Sam and Joe.

'Bow to the Queen,' said Zoe.

Joe and Sam and Dee bowed to the Queen.

'Now for the magic lemonade,' said Zoe.

She worked the handle again.

There was nothing, nothing at all.

'Oh dear,' said Zoe. 'No more magic

lemonade. I must have used it all up.

What a
splendid
idea!

Never mind. I am a very kind

queen. I am sure there is a bottle

of magic lemonade in the fridge

at home. I will go and fetch it.

Make way for the Queen!'

They all made way for the Queen. Zoe
swept past them.

'You must all bring something to eat.
That is my royal command. We will
have a royal feast in the royal pavilion!'

Zoe tottered off home. 'She's not a queen at all, grumbled Dee. 'She's a bossy boots.'

All the same she did as she said.

'What a show-off,' muttered Joe.

All the same, he did as he was told.

'She always wants to be IT,' complained

Sam, and went looking for something to eat.

Zoe returned with some magic lemonade. Joe brought raisins. Dee had biscuits. Sam had bananas. They had a wonderful feast in the royal kitchen.

'Three cheers for Queen Bossy Boots,' said Dee.

Hip-hip!

Hooray!

'Three cheers for Her Royal Show-off,' said Joe.

'Three cheers for IT!' said Sam.

43

'I am not a bossy boots,' said Zoe
taking off her cloak.

'I am not Her Royal Show-off,' she

added, taking off her crown.

'I am not IT,' she said, kicking off her

high-heeled shoes.

'I am not a queen either,' she said,

ruffling up her hair into a tangle.

'Now I am a witch! That is not magic lemonade. That is magic potion. It will turn you all into . . .

. . . FROGS!'